THE BARN

A Richard Jackson Book

THE
BARN

AVI

ORCHARD BOOKS • NEW YORK

Orchard Books
95 Madison Avenue, New York, NY 10016

Manufactured in the United States of America
Book design by Mina Greenstein
The text of this book is set in 12 point Imprint.
1   3   5   7   9   10   8   6   4   2

Library of Congress Cataloging-in-Publication Data
Avi, date.
The barn / Avi.
p.   cm.
"A Richard Jackson book"—T.p. verso.
Summary: In an effort to fulfill their dying father's last re-
quest, nine-year-old Ben and his brother and sister construct a
barn on their land in the Oregon Territory.
ISBN 0-531-06861-7.   ISBN 0-531-08711-5 (lib. bdg.)
[1. Father and child—Fiction.   2. Sick—
Fiction.   3. Building—Fiction.
4. Farm life—Fiction.]   I. Title.
PZ7.A953Bar   1994
[Fic]—dc20   94-6920

For Ashley Cross

"Your father has met with an accident."
Schoolmaster Dortmeister, his wife
by his side, spoke gravely to me in the best
parlor of their house in Portland, where I
was boarding at school. The only other
time I had seen that room was when my
father had left me there, seven months before. That was also the last time I had seen
Father.

Mrs. Dortmeister put the back of her
small hand to my cheek and said, "Benjamin, I understand it's not so very bad."

"But you're needed at home," the schoolmaster said. "Your sister has come to take
you."

Father had brought me to Portland for Mother's sake. To soothe my upset over leaving our farm, he told two tales for every mile the mule trod on the journey. He recited his best jokes, too—taking on voices, making sounds and gesturing as if he had ten tongues and fifteen hands. We were so full of our usual private mischief that I was much comforted. He promised to fetch me for a holiday in four months' time. He never came.

So of course I wanted to rush off and find Nettie; yet I would not leave the parlor without permission. They were fair in that place but strict.

"Benjamin," the schoolmaster went on, "you are the finest student I have ever had." He always called me *Benjamin*, though I preferred what my father called me: *Ben*. But that name, *Ben*, Mr. Dortmeister told me, was not dignified. He said I must put it aside since—as far as he was concerned—I was destined for higher things. "You may be only nine years old, but you're fit for more than farming. You know your letters, sums, and geometry better and are wiser than all the rest of my students combined."

Mr. Dortmeister had round gray eyes and a nose too big for his face. Tufts of hair grew out of his ears. I had always thought him comical. But when I looked up at him that time, in his best parlor, I thought he seemed about to cry.

As for me, my head was crowded with worry about Father and thoughts of Nettie, who was outside, waiting—impatiently, no doubt. At the best of times, Nettie was not a patient soul. Nothing happened fast enough for her.

Mrs. Dortmeister said, "Your sister suggests that you'll be home only a short time. So we shall look for your early return."

I replied, "I am sure I'll return," though I said it mostly because I thought that's what the schoolmaster wanted to hear.

"Do," he said. "You'll always be welcome."

I made a move to go, but Mr. Dortmeister held me by speaking again. "Benjamin," he said, "you must tell your father that I agree with him, that your gift of learning is particular fine. He will know then how truly sorry I am to lose you."

I said, "I'll tell him, sir."

"Wish your father a sound recovery. I'll retain the school fees against your return."

"Yes, sir," I said, and once again made a motion to leave.

Still, he would not release me. "Benjamin," he said, "we want to pray with you now." He and his wife bowed their heads. So I did the same.

"Our Father," the schoolmaster began, "who art in heaven, hallowed be Thy name. Thy kingdom come, Thy will be done on earth as it is in heaven.

"Amen," he ended, as did his wife.

"Amen," I echoed.

Then he sighed. "Very well, Benjamin. Your sister is waiting. We bid you farewell." Young as I was, he shook my hand, and we parted like two refined gentlemen. At last I turned and dashed away.

I found Nettie pacing up and down by our wagon. She was tall and thin with hair black as night and a sweet face that never could hide thoughts. The moment I saw her peering out from her poke bonnet, I knew Father's situation was worse than I'd been told.

This leave-taking occurred in the spring
of the year 1855, in the Willamette
Valley, Oregon Territory. Our claim was
in Yamhill County, some thirty miles from
Mr. Dortmeister's school, off the immi-
grant trails. So there was plenty of time for
Nettie to tell me on our journey home all
that had happened.

Father had been plowing with the oxen
in the west section when he took ill and
collapsed. Since my older brother, Harrison, was over by the creek using the mule
to haul stone, he had no inkling. It was
when Father did not come in for dinner

that Nettie and he began to fear something was wrong. Only after some searching did they find him stretched out on the ground.

Nettie told me that at first she thought he was dead, that we were orphans. Mother had died a year before of the diphtheria. Our brother Jefferson had died on the trail coming west.

Nettie said that though in all other ways Father appeared hardly alive, his heart was beating. Harrison heard it when he put his ear to Father's chest.

Even at thirteen, Harrison was big and strong. He was able to lift Father onto the mule. And with Nettie leading the oxen, they made for home and got Father into bed. All night they watched him. He had opened his eyes by morning. Not much more.

So Harrison rode to town for Dr. Flannagan, who came late the next night. After a study he said that Father had suffered a fit of palsy.

Sitting there in the wagon with Nettie, I felt the word "palsy" slide down my back like a cold hand. I had heard of such a thing but was not sure what it was, other than a horror.

"Nettie, what's the palsy?"

"I'm not sure," she admitted. "But Ben, I'll tell you one thing: it's as if he's not there. Most times his eyes are open. And he does move some, but only jerky. Worse, though, is when he tries to speak. I say 'try,' Ben, because it's not words he's saying, not proper ones, just gargle sounds. It's as if he's gone all to foolish."

"Nettie," I said, "is he going to live?"

At first she did not reply. Finally she answered, "The doctor said he couldn't tell. He might live for a long time, or he could die tomorrow. No saying when it might happen again."

"What might happen?"

"Another fit. But that one would be worse, because there's nothing to cure what he has—except time."

"How much time?"

"We waited a couple of days after the doctor, but there was no change. That's when Harrison and I decided you'd better come home. You're not sorry, are you?"

"No," I said.

"Father was so proud of you, Ben, for being at school. He said that's what Mother wanted."

"I know," I said. Before our mother died, she had made Father promise he would send me to Portland. I did not want to go. First he told me that such a promise was sacred and we must honor it. Then he added that since Nettie was oldest and a girl, she had to take Mother's place. And whereas Harrison was a grown boy and so strong, he was needed for fieldwork. I was the youngest and so could be spared. But I felt certain the real reason was that they all thought I was the smartest and thereby different.

"Ben," Nettie went on, "Father hadn't seemed sick at all. Nothing wrong that either of us saw. He was the usual, hardly noticing today for planning tomorrow. I mean, all he would talk about was the barn he said we'd be starting."

The idea of a barn was something I had not heard about. The oxen, along with the mule and the cow, were kept in a lean-to Father had built. We had lived in it when we'd first come to Oregon, two years before, traveling from Missouri after having lived in Vermont and in Illinois. I said, "What barn?"

"Well, Father kept saying we were ready for a real one, that our luck had finally turned." Her voice broke then.

"Nettie," I said, keeping my eyes on the rutted road, "our family doesn't seem to have much luck, does it?"

She considered awhile. Then she said, "Ben, I remember something Mother once told me about luck."

I turned. "What's that?"

"She said, 'People who talk about luck a lot don't think much of themselves.' "

"Father always talks about luck."

"Ben . . ."

"What?"

"I think that's why she said it."

We reached home in the late afternoon of the second day. Harrison was waiting for us. In the seven months since I'd last seen him, he appeared to have grown about a foot. How I envied his size and strength, his shovel-wide face and those hands as tough as horn. But though Harrison was as big as I was small, his eyes were like a deer's, always seeming to ask permission. I could tell he was glad to see us.

"Any better?" were Nettie's first words.

"No," Harrison told her.

For a moment we just stood there, the

three of us. We hardly knew what or how to be.

Then Nettie said, "Better go inside."

The house was the second one Father had built in Oregon Territory. It was not much more than a single large room made from ash tree logs. Most folks used pine, but pine grew huge, so it took more work, and Father was in a hurry.

The roof was made with bark shakes. The dirt floor was kept strewn with fresh grass during wet times. Harrison had the job of keeping the inside walls daubed with clay to hold the weather out, a constant task.

When Father first built it, the house had been sweet and clean, but hearth smoke had turned the walls all gray and streaked. That hearth never did draw proper, though Father fussed and fussed with it. Each time he gave up, he would say to me, "Ben, I've been thinking. Maybe it would be a good thing to keep the smoke in here." And I would say, "Why?" And his answer was always, "You know, smoke so confuses a mosquito, he'll bite another mosquito before he bites us." I'd laugh at that every time. Anyway, the smoke did cut back on the bugs.

There were two windows, each stretched over with scraped elk hide to allow in pale light. There was a loft where Harrison and I slept and—between the windows—a shelf that held our Bible, Mother's copy of *Pilgrim's Progress*, and a book of sewing patterns.

Father's big bed had a straw mattress that crinkled like a kindling fire when he moved about on it. Nettie's place was at the other end of the room. Because she was a girl, it was curtained with canvas from our old wagon.

Most of our furnishings had been brought from back East. There was Mother's great chest, which still held her dresses. (Father said he was saving them for Nettie, but she said she never would put them on. "If you wear your mother's dresses, you get your mother's life" was the way she put it. And Father replied, "She got me, didn't she?" which made me grin, though Nettie frowned.)

Also, we had a table that Grandfather had made as Mother's wedding gift. And five chairs, one for each family member. Four were around the table, one against the wall. That was Mother's. Of all the things we owned, I liked these chairs best because Harrison had made them.

In one corner stood an old floor clock from my father's side of the family. I cannot recall it ever working. Harrison would have tried fixing it, but Father always said that *he* was Father Time, so the clock was his to tinker with. He had a joke for that, too, saying he planned on finding a way to get time to run backward since, he said, he'd made a couple of mistakes in his life, but now that he'd practiced some, he was bound to get things right.

Though the clock never did move off two-eighteen, it still was the finest thing our family owned and thus took the pride of corner place.

That was our home.

When I came in through the door, I was shocked by the smell, like an open privy. Alarmed, I looked over to Harrison.

"He doesn't have much control," he said, his voice low.

Nettie gave me a tap and a little push. "Go on up to him," she said.

It was then I had my first look at Father as he had become. He lay on the big bed, back propped against the wall. He was fully dressed—faded blue-striped flannel shirt, wool trousers—though his boots were off. His hard hands lay by his sides like soft slabs of clay.

The last time I had seen him, he was tall and strong. The only thing he'd never owed money on, he'd say, was his handsome face, and Mother bought it right off the shelf.

Now that same face showed nothing but sick and sour dirtiness. His beard—about which he'd been so vain and about which I had teased him often in fun—was all crossways, as was his gray-streaked hair.

He made me think of an old corn husk doll without stuffing. As I stood staring, he made fluttering motions at the coverlet, his fingers jumping like small fish hauled to land.

Nettie whispered, "Go closer. But mind . . . he won't hardly notice."

I went up to his bed.

"Father!" Nettie said, though it was not normal speaking. She spoke loud and hard, the way you gee up a mule. "Ben's come!"

Father just lay there. Then came jerks of his fingers, causing the mattress to crackle. Finally he opened his lips, and a sound came out. It was not words like people speak, but something squeezed from his throat, thick and mangled. Worse, spit spilled from one corner of his mouth and trickled into his beard.

As for those eyes, which once had teased and laughed so with me, they had become as deep as a well that sank forever, only to fetch up dry.

That night the three of us, Harrison, Nettie, and I, sat at the table. Nettie had cooked up some potatoes, and we had them with milk. She and Harrison hardly asked about my schooling, though I did tell them Mr. Dortmeister had kept the fees against my return. Mostly we talked about what we should do for Father. I don't know if he could hear us or even hear at all, but it seemed proper to keep our voices low. Perhaps we were afraid someone would hear, though our nearest neighbors—the Gartells—were six miles away and stand-offish at any rate.

"You're the oldest boy," Nettie said to

Harrison. "It's for you to make the decisions."

He shook his head. "You're two years older than me."

She said, "But I might get married."

I was surprised.

Harrison nodded. "Tod Buckman has been sparking her."

"You going to leave?" I asked Nettie.

She smiled some. "I don't know. Mr. Buckman asked . . . at Christmastime. Father made no objections, save that we wait. Well, I wasn't going to wait, but now . . ." She turned back to Harrison. "Still, it's up to you," she insisted.

Harrison dipped his head. "Nettie, I can't do it."

"Do what?" I asked.

"Keep up the claim. We've got to stay two more years before it's ours."

"We'll be here," I said. I looked at Nettie. "Won't we?"

She said, "I don't know."

Then no one spoke for a while.

"Maybe he'll get better," I finally said with a glance over my shoulder at Father.

When they did not reply, I went on: "It's only a sickness."

Harrison and Nettie exchanged a look that I could not understand.

"Ben . . . ," Nettie said.

"What?"

"I want you to feed Father."

"Why? Can't he—?" I didn't finish the sentence. Instead I turned and gazed at Father again.

"Go on," Nettie urged. "Do it."

I got up, fetched his bowl, filled it, then took it and a spoon to where he lay. As I drew closer, I saw his eyes flick back and forth over me. Deep as they were, this time I could see they had points of light in them, like distant stars. The sight startled me. But he shifted, and I saw that the light was no more than a reflection of the embers in the hearth.

"Father," I asked, "do you want to eat?"

Other than a few finger twitches, he made no response.

"Ben," Nettie said, "you have to be louder."

I drew breath. "Do you want to eat?" I

cried out, feeling shame to yell at him that way.

Father opened his mouth a tad, and some of those awful sounds came forth.

I dipped my spoon into the bowl, scooped up a potato bit, and held it out toward him. I guess I expected him to lean forward. When he did not, I moved closer, inching the spoon near his mouth. There was some twitching in his face but not much else.

I put the spoon to his lips—his mouth was half-open—I don't know why, but so was mine—and tried to tip the potato in. The piece tumbled down his front.

I shrank back, mortified. It took a while before I was able to look at him again. Those eyes of his just blinked.

I plucked up the potato bit and tried to set it right in his mouth, like a bird doing for its chicks. I almost had to force it in. Doing so made me sick to my stomach.

Then I stood back, stared down into the bowl, and used my spoon to mash the potato to make a sort of gruel. I fed that to him with more success, but it took a long time. As much dribbled down into his beard as got inside him. It was necessary to wipe him off time and time again.

When I finally returned to the table—where Harrison and Nettie had been looking on in silence—I was exhausted. I bowed my head in my arms and commenced to tremble.

Nettie touched me. "You see," she said.

But I flung myself away and stood outside. The sky was dark and immense. The stars were far. And I felt so small.

L ater that night, in the loft, Harrison reached over and touched my head. "Ben," he whispered, "I'm glad you're home. Father was late with planting. Nettie and I needed you here."

"Harrison," I said, "I can work the fields, too."

He said nothing.

"I can," I insisted.

"Ben," he finally replied, "whatever you do will be a help."

After a while I said, "Harrison, how come he never fetched me home for a holiday?" I had to ask him twice.

At last he said, "Father believed that

school would make you so different, you'd not be happy here."

"That's not true!"

"Said he'd build a big barn so you'd have something fine to come home to."

6

Early next morning, in air cool enough for our breaths to cloud, Harrison and I pulled the ox team from the lean-to.

The lean-to was cut into a low hill and had been made quickly from already fallen trees so we could have a roof above our heads when we took up the claim. Later, after Father built the log house, we began to keep the oxen, mule, and cow there, but it was now in sad repair and leaked badly. No doubt that was why Father had been talking of a real barn.

That first day, we led the oxen to the west field, the section where Father had taken ill. Harrison hitched up the plow, which was not much, mostly wood, with just a repaired strip of iron for a blade edge.

I never saw anyone work so hard as Harrison. But big as he was, he had nothing on Father's skill for plowing deep. And though that field had been plowed before, it was not yet kind. I had to follow behind and break clods with the ax.

Nettie stayed to home with Father and did chores, coming out only to bring us our midday food.

"How is he?" Harrison asked.

"The same," she replied as though a lament.

By the end of the day, what we accomplished was hardly done proper, but it was something. Harrison said it was good enough to seed.

It was near dark when he and I returned to the house. Then, while the three of us sat around the table and ate our potatoes and milk, Nettie announced, "We can't do it this way."

Harrison lifted his head. "Do what?"

"Me tending Father all the days."

"Why not?" Harrison asked. He was not angry. He just wanted to know.

"I'll go mad," Nettie told him.

He gazed at her.

"Or leave," she added.

Harrison turned back to his food.

"We could take turns," I said after a while. "Each day one of us will stay with him. That way it will be only once in every three days for each of us."

"Fine," Nettie said quickly.

Harrison looked at us. "All right."

I said, "Each evening we can agree about what's to be done and divide it up. I'll be the one to tend him tomorrow."

Harrison considered me for a moment, then reached out a big hand and gave my head a shake. "You *are* the smart one."

Nettie nodded. "Always was."

"Like Father used to say, you're fit for more than here."

My brother's words made me think of Mr. Dortmeister, but I said nothing back.

Next morning, just before Harrison and Nettie left, she said, "Father needs to be fed and cleaned."

"Cleaned?"

"When he fouls himself."

I started to protest, but Nettie cut me short. "Ben," she said, "this was your idea. And a good one." Then they went. And there I was, alone with Father for the first time. Realizing that I had to clean him made me sick.

I remained at the table, only now and again turning to look at Father propped up on his bed. Once in a while his mattress crackled, an irritating sound. The truth is, I hardly had to look; he smelled that bad. And those eyes of his seemed to be looking here, there, everywhere.

I don't know why, but all of a sudden I came to think of him as a cave—a deep, dark cave. And there was an animal—of some kind—inside it, inside *him*, hiding. It might have been a possum. Or a mountain lion. I could see nothing in that cave of him but those animal eyes. Yet I had to approach the cave. Had to go into it. I could hardly move from the table. I felt like a wheel without spokes.

I must talk about this matter of Father's foulness. It needs to be said and understood, then be done with.

He, who had been a clean man, now had no control. Any skunk smelled sweeter.

That morning, when, for the first time, I approached him about this, I gagged. Once—as I set to the necessary work—I ran from the house and vomited. For there I was, nine years of age, having to undress my father and clean his privates both back and front. What shame I felt that *he* should be like a baby to *me*, who was his youngest son!

Aside from the filth, it was hard work,

for it was then that I learned how truly helpless Father had become. I had to push and shove and twist him around. It was loathsome, painful work to make him decent.

And yet . . . and yet it is this I have to say: for all the horror of it that first time, cleaning Father was to become as normal and simple as grass growing. Indeed, we three never spoke of it again—nor will I here. But it took its place as part of our lives—day in and day out—as long as we were together.

The truth is, his filth proved that Father still lived. Thus it was to become not dirt but something of the life that we struggled to hold in this mortal world.

In this way did I begin to learn how heaven and earth do mingle.

8

Once I had cleaned Father that morning, I fed him—or tried to. As before, only half the food that went into his mouth stayed. His own tongue seemed too thick and heavy for him. He could not use it properly and appeared to chew it as much as the potato. Just to swallow was a struggle. I found myself with a spoon in one hand and a cloth in the other to wipe him again and again.

That done, I went about drawing water from the creek, hauling wood, splitting it, stacking it, making the house somewhat clean, milking the cow, working the small garden ground that was close by. I also brought in potatoes from the food cellar, cooked them, and at midday carried them out to Nettie and Harrison.

Harrison said, "How is he?"

"The same," I replied.

Then I looked over the field, and I saw that they had plowed twice as much as Harrison and I had done.

Once I hurried back to Father, I began to think that I'd been wrong to suggest changing our work each day. For what I saw was this: it would be better if it were me who always stayed home.

That night, as we ate our dinner, I said, "You two can do more work outside without me. I should be the one to be here."

"That wouldn't be fair," Nettie said.

I answered, "But it's true."

"To stay in, day after day, would make me crazed," she whispered.

Harrison studied me. "Is that what you really want?" he asked.

"The planting and fieldwork have to come first," I reasoned.

Nettie said, "You have to promise to say when it gets too hard."

"I will."

"Well, then, if you want it," she said.

Harrison nodded his agreement.

9

For Father and me, the next three days were much the same as our first. Nettie and Harrison tilled the fields. I stayed home and worked there but mostly looked after Father, feeding him, cleaning him.

It was like keeping watch on an empty box. At some points I took out my school reader and sat by the door and tried to study it. The task seemed to be from another life. Besides, I found myself continually looking around to Father. He gave nothing back.

Once or twice I thought—from his stillness—that he had died. Each time my heart froze. Then I saw that I was wrong and was ashamed of myself for giving way so easily.

Nettie had removed Father's chair from the table. Now and again I would set it by the side of his bed and read him some passages from *Pilgrim's Progress*. Mother had often read it to us. Father liked to listen. But now it was impossible for me to know whether or not he could understand the words.

It was during the fourth day when, as I sat reading to him, I observed that his eyes had shifted toward me. After a time I decided he was actually looking at me.

I looked back but, seeing nothing there, felt a rage of discouragement, which I hated.

For a while we stared at each other. "Do you know me?" I finally said. I spoke in that loud voice that was so unnatural and made me feel as though I were talking to a dumb beast. But when you talk to a mule, you know it is a mule. This was my father.

There was some fluttering of his hands, small movements of muscles in his face.

And those eyes—empty, watery eyes—all they did was twitch. No more.

Frustrated, I got up and stood by the door to stare out. Our claim, which was all the land that I could see—three hundred and twenty acres—stretched before me. It was clear that day, the sky high with the valley clouds that were, as Mother once said, like feather beds for angels. The eastern mountains—beyond some low hills—were streaked with snow. The western mountains glowered in shadow. Down by the creek I could just see the tops of the trees. In the first blush of spring, the leaves made a green mist. Birds, ever mindless, flew by. It was all open, free, and fair but without any shape or design that I could see. What, I wondered, would become of us?

I forced myself back into our house, so dim, closed, and bad smelling. Once again I took up my place by him.

"Father!" I shouted. "I am Ben, your son!"

He gave no more answer to my words than he had before.

"Shall I talk to you?" I said.

His eyes moved.

Not knowing what else to do, but wanting so much to find a way to fill the time, I began to tell him about Mr. Dortmeister's school and all that was taught there. I even read Father some of my schoolbook. But his eyes did little more than dart this way and that.

I tried telling him some of his own favorite jokes, ones that he had told no one but me. I even made myself laugh. But I might as well have been counting seeds. He showed as much emotion as a stone in the field.

Feeling lost, I went out to the cow and talked to her and scratched her ears. Of a sudden she turned around and butted my face. That a cow could respond more than my father made my heart swell with pain, and in my anger I struck her on her rump.

Then I rebuked myself for such thoughts and actions and once again returned to the house and took up my place by Father's bed.

His eyes had turned almost lively. He opened his mouth, and one of his strange sounds sputtered out. The spit came, too, and made his beard glisten.

I sat up and gaped at him, not certain if I was seeing something different. "Are you trying to talk?" I demanded.

When he made no further response, my momentary excitement crumpled to naught.

Frightened that I could find nothing more to tell him, I walked around the house, fetched some potatoes, and thought to cut them up. But I left them on the table and turned back to Father. I had come up with something to say.

"Nettie," I shouted at him. "Nettie told me you were planning to build a barn! A real barn to show our luck had turned!"

The moment I said that, I realized how sinful I was being, as if I were mocking him. Of course there was no reaction. Not at first. But then his mouth opened and his eyes shifted. We stared at each other for a long time. How strange his eyes seemed.

They were brown, flecked with tiny spots of gold, the pupils black and enlarged to let in such light as there was.

Again I had the sense that I was looking into a cave. What was I seeing inside now?

I leaned forward. Our faces were but inches apart. "Father!" I shouted. "Nettie told me you were planning to build a barn! A real one! Is that true?"

He gazed dumbly at me.

"Father!" I shouted again. "If you *were* thinking of a barn—*close* your eyes! Close your eyes!"

There was some movement of muscle and a raspy gargle from his throat. Something twitched around his mouth, too, but those eyes remained staring wide and empty.

Suddenly all my anger rushed together within my chest. It was as if I had been struck by a musket ball. Why had he done this? It was a cruel thing he had become, and I felt a hatred for it. He had abandoned us when we needed him. He had become a child when *we* were the children. He had failed us. Oh, I so wanted to strike him and make him feel my pain.

"Father!" I screamed in annoyance. "If you mean *yes*, you *must* close your eyes!"

And then—he did.

When I realized he had given me an answer, I was so stunned I burst into tears.

IO

I tore out to the field. "Father spoke to me!" I cried to Nettie and Harrison. "Father spoke to me!"

They stopped work instantly.

"What do you mean?" Nettie said as I ran up to them, breathless.

I managed to say, "I—I asked him a question and—and he said yes."

Harrison's eyes widened. "What was the question?"

"I asked if he was going to build a barn."

"He *said* yes?" Nettie demanded. They stared at me in disbelief.

"Well, it was not exactly *saying*," I admitted. "But he meant it, Nettie. He did."

"If he wasn't *saying*, Ben," she wanted to know, "what *was* he doing?"

"He spoke with his eyes."

The two of them exchanged looks. "Ben," Nettie snapped with crossness, "what kind of fool thing are you trying to do?" It was the first harsh word that I'd heard from her since I had come home.

"He can talk with his eyes," I cried. "He can! I saw him. He really did!"

"Never knew any living creature could talk with its eyes," Harrison said.

I said, "Just come and see for yourself. Please."

Nettie would have none of it. "Ben, we've work to do. How can you stand there and tell us he did things like that? It's not natural."

"But he *did*," I cried.

"This something you learned in school?" Harrison's voice was not pleasant.

I took hold of his arm. "Harrison," I begged, "please come. *Please*."

He shook my hand off, and they looked at each other a second time.

It was Nettie, as usual, who decided.

"Just this once. But Ben, I'll go hard on you if you're fooling. I will."

They left the oxen with the plow to show me they believed nothing of what I had told them. But still, they came back to the house and stood on either side of Father's bed.

He was, as always, looking empty, though his eyes were moving, moving. For a while we gazed at him.

"He seems the same to me," Harrison finally said.

"Wait," I told him. Then I drew the chair up as I had done before. Kneeling on it, I leaned close. "Father!" I shouted. "It's me, Ben!"

Father's fingers twitched some. And his feet stirred a bit.

"Ben," Nettie said, "this is foolishness."

"Wait!" I shouted, but at them, not at Father. "Father!" I cried anew, and I stretched out my hand toward Nettie. "This is Nettie. If you know her, blink your eyes!"

His eyes shifted, his tongue flopped, and

spit bubbled from his mouth. I wondered if I had been mistaken.

Harrison turned away. "I have work to do," he said.

"Father!" I screamed. "Show Nettie that you know it's her! That you know your daughter! Close your eyes! Close them to show you know!"

And he did.

There was a silence in the house as big as any sky. Nettie, her voice suddenly in tatters, whispered, "Ben, that doesn't *mean*. It's only wishing."

I turned back to Father. "Show them again, Father!" I shouted. "Close your eyes to say you know it's your Nettie standing there."

Once again he closed his eyes.

"Oh, mercy . . . ," Nettie murmured.

"Now blink if you see Harrison, Father. I want you to do it for him! *Please!* For Harrison. Tell him you know him. Go on!"

Father blinked.

Nettie gasped, covered her face with her

hands. Harrison stared, his mouth agape. I clapped my hands with glee.

And that was how I came to know that the creature within the cave was Father himself.

II

For dinner that night, I served up potatoes in our regular fashion. But while I'd been preparing them, I'd been thinking. Before we sat down, I said, "I think we should bring Father to the table."

That startled Nettie. "What do you mean?" she asked.

Even Harrison looked queerly at me. "He can't sit," he said.

But I said, "We can tie him to his chair."

Harrison turned to Nettie in dismay. Her face had gone a chalky white. "Ben," she breathed, "that can't be right. It can't."

"We'll ask him," I answered. Before they could object, I ran over to the bed. "Father!" I shouted—and by now you know that whenever anyone talked to him it was by shouting—"Do you want to come to the table? Do you? Blink your eyes!"

He did.

"There," I said in triumph. "He said yes."

They hardly knew what to say.

"Do you mind being tied?" I asked him. "Do you?"

He just gazed at me, eyes wide.

"There," I cried. "He's saying no."

"Ben . . . ," Nettie said, all flustered. "Are you really sure?"

"Yes!" I shouted. "Yes!"

Nettie hesitated no more. She pulled Father's chair back to the table, then ran for some rope. Harrison, meanwhile, came to Father's bed and, after stopping for a moment, picked him up, carried him over, then set him down. Nettie ran the rope about his chest and stomach. I tied it up behind.

Finally we three sat at our places. It was as if we had brought in a scarecrow from the fields and propped him up for company. But then Father opened his mouth and gurgled. I clapped my hands.

"Ben!" Nettie cried in fear.

"No, look," I insisted. "He's glad."

She turned to look. Father was blinking his eyes.

Harrison threw back his head and let out a whoop.

I started to put Father's plate before him, but Nettie snatched it back. "Ben, he can't," she pleaded. "It's too hard."

I let it be.

At last we fell to eating, and it was more like old times, with noise and messiness. And all the while Father sat there. Sometimes he shifted about or made his gargle sounds. Or blinked. Now and again I fed him.

But halfway through the dinner, his head drooped forward. On the instant, our happiness fled.

"What's happened?" Harrison said to me, as if I could explain all things about Father.

"I don't know," I admitted.

"I think he's asleep," Nettie said. "Exhausted from saying yes."

I grinned with pleasure. Harrison nodded.

The three of us worked to get him out of the chair and back in his bed.

Softly, so as not to have him notice, we returned to the table.

"This mean he's getting better?" Harrison wondered out loud.

"I hope. . . ."

Nettie said, "Maybe he could do that blinking before, and we just didn't notice."

"It took Ben to think of it," Harrison said.

"No," I answered, "Nettie's right. We're going to have to watch and find out if he can do more."

But when I turned back to Father, he lay asleep, as still as a field in winter.

12

Over the next few days, it became certain that Father was answering yes-or-no questions with his eyes, that he could, in his fashion, understand and be with us. During the days, he became almost a comfort to me.

However, yes blinks and no looks only went so far. The plain truth was, there were no more improvements. And he was growing thinner all the time.

One rainy day, three weeks after I'd come home, I was in the house alone with Father. As I recollect, the rain was not so hard as to keep Harrison and Nettie in. They and the oxen were at work felling trees. With Father abed, we used the fire more, and wood was low. I was sitting by Father's bed, trying to read him some of *Pilgrim's Progress*. Wind gusts beat down the chimney and made the house smoky. The light was dull, and it was difficult to read. Besides, I still knew nothing of what he took from my efforts.

Our roof was thick enough, but here and there it leaked some. From time to time I stuck plugs of grass into the cracks. After a while I naturally thought of the lean-to. Knowing it leaked worse than the house, I said to Father, "I'm going to patch the roof of the lean-to. Do you understand?"

He blinked his understanding.

I found it was not just the roof that leaked but the walls as well. The cow and mule were standing deep in mud—which is bad for their hooves—and kept shifting about to avoid the seeping wet.

I brought in some grass to soak up the rain under their feet and began to plug the lean-to roof. The plugging worked well enough, but I saw how poor that place had become. I suppose that's what made me think more about a barn.

Father had been talking about a barn before he was struck. And it was mention of a barn that allowed me to see he could understand us and give answers with his eyes. Suddenly it came to me how I might be able to stir life back into him.

I ran to the house to sit with Father again. I was dripping wet but paid no mind. He was staring straight ahead into the gloom. Gathering up my courage, I said, "Father, we need a new barn, don't we?"

He shifted and after a few moments gave the yes sign with his eyes. He tried to talk, and I could see that his fingers grew uncommon agitated.

Encouraged, I cried, "Father, that barn is *very* important to you, isn't it?"

Again, his reply was yes.

"Can you tell me how important?" I said, trying to push him on.

For a response he only gaped at me. But I would not give up. I fetched the lamp, lit it, and set it down so we could see each other clearly. Then, once again, I tried: "Father, how *important* is it to *you* that we have a *new* barn? You *must* find a way to *tell* me."

His eyes blinked some, but I wanted more.

"*Show* me how important!" I demanded. "You've got to."

He opened his mouth and made his sounds. But that was nothing new. I shook my head and cried, "I need *more*!"

He shut his eyes. His body tightened. His feet twitched. His fingers fluttered. It was like some strong man preparing to lift a huge load. In fact, what he did was jerk his right hand up. In fairness it was hardly more than an inch. But I could not have read him more plainly if he had written it out.

From that moment on, I was certain I had found the way to bring him back to life: we would build him a barn.

13

I had refueled the lamp when Harrison and Nettie came in. They were both exhausted and hungry. Even so, as he did every night, Harrison stood by Father and told him what he'd done. After Nettie changed to dry clothes, she did the same.

When we set to dinner, I had Father brought to the table and tied into his chair. That was no longer uncommon, and Harrison and Nettie made little of it. But then, in the midst of their chatter, I said, "I have found a way to cure Father."

The house felt as silent as the moon.

At last Nettie said, "What are you talking about?"

I cleared my throat and said, "Father told me some things today."

"*Told?*" she said.

"Yes."

"*Things?*" Harrison asked. "With his eyes?"

"More than that," I answered. "With his hand. He signaled me."

Nettie put down her spoon. "What did you think he was saying?"

"He was telling me what was most important to him. I read him like a book."

The moment I said that, I knew it was wrong to use those words. Nettie gave a frown; then the two of them studied Father for a moment. Finally Nettie turned to me and said, "Ben, I don't believe you."

So I got up, leaned over behind Father, and said, "Father, you told me what's important to you, didn't you?"

He blinked his yes.

"See!" I cried.

"Well, what is it?" Nettie demanded sharply.

I said, "He wants us to build a new barn."

Harrison considered me with astonishment, whistled, then shook his head. Nettie stood and walked away. We watched her as she paced in agitation.

"Why shouldn't we?" I asked them both at once.

Nettie said at last, "Put Father back to bed and we'll talk."

"But it's what he wants us to do," I insisted. "It will cure him! He told me."

"Ben!" she said in a hard voice. "Do what I say!"

Harrison put Father back to bed. I pulled up his coverlet and came back to the table. But no, Nettie would have us go outside, which we did.

The earth smelled ripe. Now and again the wind blew in like the wheeze of an old horse. The rain had eased off to little more than a fog, so there were no stars. There was just the glow of yellow light from the window to give the three of us faces. Nettie, I saw, was angry.

"Look here, Ben," she began. "This won't do."

"What won't do?"

"It's what Mother once told me: 'A gift in dead hands is water in a broken jug.' "

To which I exclaimed, "He's not dead!"

Nettie shook her head. "It's all very well your saying you read him like a book. We know how good you read. We know how school smart you are. That's why Father sent you there. But Ben, there are times I think you're the only one writing that book."

I said, "I don't understand."

"Ben," she cried, "you're having him tell you things you *want* him to say!"

"That's not true!" I cried.

Nettie took me by the shoulders and gave me a shake. "Father won't live, Ben. He won't! Can't you see it's only a matter of time? He's wasting away. Don't you know that?"

"He *can* live," I threw back. "But he wants something to live for."

"It's just *your* wanting, Ben—that's all! Look here," she said. "I'm not going to stop in this place forever. I mean to marry. I do. Then I'll go off. And you, you're for school and being educated."

"I won't go back!" I declared.

"Oh, Ben, you must."

"What about Harrison?" I asked.

"I don't know," Harrison said for himself. "Building a barn would be a lot of work. I mean, a barn is as much as saying we're going to keep this claim. But if you go, and Nettie goes, there's no saying where I'll be. Not likely here."

"Father wants it," I said again.

"Ben, that's *forever* talk," Nettie declared. "We don't have time for forever."

Harrison nodded his agreement.

"But if Father *does* die," I cried out, "he *would* be here forever. Like Mother."

Nettie turned away. "That can't make a difference," she said.

"But maybe," I pleaded, "that's why he wants the barn. It might be something to stay with *him*."

"Ben!" Nettie faced me again. "You're not a part of this. You were meant to go off and be different. To *be* somebody. Not like us."

On the instant, I tore into her, flailing away with my fists, crying, "I am like you.

I am!" Harrison leaped and hauled me away, smothering me in his arms, though I kept crying, "I'm the same as you! The same!"

When he let me go, I spun about, wanting to confront Nettie again, but she had marched off into the fog. I pulled Harrison back into the house. "You ask Father," I insisted. "For yourself."

Harrison stood over him, the lamplight causing a shadow that made him appear even bigger than he was. Father looked smaller.

At first Harrison just stood there, his hands working. "Father!" he finally shouted. But instead of trying more, he merely shrugged. "Ben, I'm no good at this. Not the way you are." He climbed up to the loft and flung himself onto his mattress.

I remained alone with Father. "I'm the same," I said to him. "I am. Say yes with your eyes or your hand. Say it!"

But he was asleep.

14

Next morning Nettie packed a satchel, saying she needed to think some. She was gone two days, and when she came back, Tod Buckman was with her. He was twenty-two years of age and worked a claim with his family ten miles to the south. He was tall, lean, and strong.

Nettie, her face stiff as planking, told us, "Tod Buckman and I are going to be married."

"When?" Harrison asked, not looking at Tod but at Nettie.

"When we can," she said.

I went to her. "You're our only sister," I said.

Her eyes were grave; her mouth worked. She said, "And I will always be."

Tod, grinning, put his arm around Nettie's waist then, looked down at me, and said, "What's more, Ben, I intend to be her only husband."

Nettie tried to hold back, but she turned all red and sputtered with laughter.

"There, Ben," Harrison said with a poke. "Only Tod can make her laugh like that." Tod laughed himself.

Nettie took Tod into the house to see Father. When he came back out, hat in hand, his smile was gone. For a moment he just stood there.

Harrison said, "What do you think?"

Tod looked to Nettie, then to Harrison and me. He said, "I'd say he's lucky having you for family."

From then on I liked Tod. And I knew, too, that Nettie would not desert us. She was just looking to get some breath of her own. Right away I began to think about the barn again.

But that night Nettie said to me, "Now, Ben, don't misunderstand my staying. If there's to be a barn, it has to be a family decision—not just yours—to build it."

I started to argue, but she would not hear a word. She was that set against it.

It made me realize that if I were going to get her to change her mind—Harrison's mind, too, perhaps—I'd have to get Father's help.

A few days later, at dinner, I said, "Now that the rain has let up, I think we should take Father out some."

"How, Ben?" Nettie asked. She was not objecting.

I said, "If Harrison could put a higher back to the barrow, we could ride him about."

"That's easy," Harrison said. By the next day, it was done. He fixed a slab of wood upright on the front of the barrow. Nettie laid out some straw on the bottom. Then Harrison pulled on Father's boots, carried him outside, and set him down in the barrow with his back propped against the slab.

Father was so thin now, the task was not hard. I tied him in.

"Do you want to see what we've done?" I shouted.

He blinked yes.

"Where to?" Harrison asked.

"We can show him how the fields look," I suggested.

Harrison took up the handles, and we started off, with Nettie and me running on either side to make sure Father did not tip out.

First we wheeled him to the section where he'd had his fit. We had put in wheat there. Our work looked like snake trails more than decent furrows, but the crop was up, looking Irish green and tasting sweet.

Harrison turned the barrow around so Father could see what we'd done.

"Planted!" Harrison shouted. "We've planted it!"

The muscles in Father's face twitched, and he made small sounds. There were a few blinks, too.

"He likes it," Harrison exclaimed. I could see he was proud.

"Show him the rest that you did," I suggested. "I'm going back to the house." They were surprised. I drew them both aside. "When I'm gone," I told them, "I want you to ask him about the barn, so I'm not part of it." Before they could object, I went off.

They returned two hours later. Harrison got Father back into bed. He had fallen asleep.

I was hoping Nettie would say something, but she did not. Unable to stop myself, I burst out, "Did you ask him?"

Harrison looked to Nettie.

"Did you?" I asked again.

"Yes," Nettie said.

"What happened?"

Harrison answered, "We took him around like you said and showed him the fields. Then when we came back, we went by the lean-to. He started fussing up, all on his own, so we stopped. That's when I asked him if he thought we should build that barn he'd been talking about."

"What did he say?"

Harrison said, "He got to moving about
. . . as if he were excited."

Nettie, looking more weary than anything, said, "He said yes."

"How?"

"He lifted his hand. This much."

My heart was pounding. "Well?" I demanded.

"I'm willing," Harrison replied.

I turned to Nettie. "What about you?"

At first she didn't answer. She went to
the fire, kneeled before it, and poked it,
stirring the embers till a lick of flame
spurted. Then she said, "Father said he
wants it."

"And?"

She sighed, stood up, and faced me. "I'll
go along."

I could not help myself. I went up to her
and gave her a hug. It was Father himself
who had convinced them.

16

"You really think it should be made of pine logs?" Harrison asked.

"It'll last that way," I told him.

Nettie said, "But it will take a lot more time to do."

"We can work harder," I said.

"We do work hard," Harrison let me know.

"But this is different," I insisted. "It's going to make Father better. You saw how just the talk of the barn helped him."

"Oh, Ben," Nettie pleaded, "don't your eyes ever see what you *don't* want to see? He's getting down to nothing!"

No one spoke. Then Harrison said, "I

suppose we could build another lean-to. That would go up fast."

I said, "It'll be the same coming down."

"Ben," Nettie cried in exasperation, "you have an answer for everything!"

I appealed to Harrison. "You're the boss builder," I said. "What do you think?"

He said, "Depends on how big it gets to be. And where it is."

The following day the three of us went out to decide where we should build the barn. There was not much disagreement. We found a pretty place near enough to our house. It was on somewhat higher ground, too, so the rain would run off.

"Could set one corner right here," Harrison said, jamming down a heel.

I ran to get a stick and stuck it in; then Nettie tapped it down with our ax.

"Should be foursquare," Harrison said. "That's the only way."

"Father lost his compass," Nettie reminded us.

"We can line it up proper at night," I said.

They looked at me, puzzled.

"It's something Schoolmaster Dortmeister taught me."

When night came—after checking Father to see that he was comfortable—I fetched a long rope, the ax, and another stick. Then the three of us went out to the stake. It was a clear night, with countless stars as though a big hand had sowed light instead of wheat.

I tied the rope to the stake. "We need the North Star," I said.

The three of us stood there then, gazing up and around to what we knew was north.

Nettie caught it first. "There!" It was about midpoint between the ground and the top of the sky.

Then I moved off from the stake, hauling back on the attached rope but always keeping it in line with the North Star. When I reached the end of the line, I laid the rope down.

SOUTH
STAKE

"There," I said, as I marked the southern end with the other stick. "That's our north-south line. We'll do the rest tomorrow."

Next day, we did more of what I had been taught in geometry. I took that rope and tied twelve knots as close to one foot apart as I could.

Then I fastened the rope to the south stake and drew it out a distance of four knots along the north-south line. At that fourth knot I changed direction, heading somewhat southeast, measuring out a five-knot length.

Holding the rope taut, I stretched it on the ground and bent the final three-knot piece so it came back to the stake.

| *

SOUTH | . .
STAKE | . . .
      . .
     . .
      .

At the stake, then, was a perfect right angle for the first corner of the barn.

Starting from the stake and using the rope to keep things straight, I marked out thirty feet on the four-foot side, twenty feet on the three-foot side. At the end of each I put down new stakes.

Using those new stakes as starting points, plus the lines I had just drawn, I laid out two other triangles.

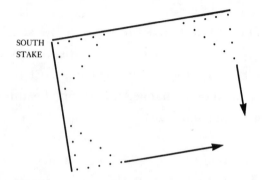

That gave us three corners.

For the fourth I extended lines from the second and third and got a decent-size rectangle.

"Ben," Harrison said, "someday you'll be governor of Oregon Territory."

By this time he was all for wanting the barn big, though Nettie—it was no surprise—argued for small. I fetched up with the idea that the rectangle we had already measured might be good enough, and we agreed to that. It was not to be the biggest barn in the territory. But a barn it would be.

Excited that we had agreed, I said, "We must tell Father."

"Not me," Nettie said.

"You be the one to tell him," I said to Harrison.

"Come with me," he said.

Harrison and I went into the house and approached the bed. I saw Father's eyes shift.

"We marked out the barn," Harrison announced.

We stood there, waiting for a response. None came.

Harrison turned to me. "I think he only listens to you," he said, and turned to walk away. I held him back.

Leaning over Father, I shouted, "We'll promise you the barn if you promise you'll get better."

His eyes moved a little.

"Do you have an answer?" I cried.

Father's hand stirred.

"There," I said to Harrison, "we've made an agreement."

Though there were hills to the east, our land ran mostly to flat. It also dipped off some toward the southwest corner. There was a creek down there—Corbs Creek—which ran good, sweet water. We would have lived closer, but the last two times Father tried building near to a creek, we were flooded out. After that, he swore he would only walk to water, not swim through it.

But Corbs Creek was the reason all the trees—pine, oak, fir, ash—grew well. They were not so old, either, because the Indians used to burn the area to keep it clear for hunting.

Again we talked of the best wood to use. I repeated that pine was what most people chose, because it would last.

"Ben," Nettie said, "with all your talk of forever, you'll have to become a preacher."

In the end Harrison agreed with me, saying we should do it right.

And so we began the barn.

We decided that each day Harrison and Nettie would come back from fieldwork earlier than usual. Then I'd go out with one of them down along the creek bottom. I would bring the ax. Whoever came with me would lead the oxen.

Once there, we'd scout around for a pine tree we could use. We needed straightness but a trunk not so big we couldn't manage to move it. As soon as we picked a tree, I'd start to chop it down. Or try to. During that time, I broke three ax handles. Harrison had to shape new ones.

When I tired, the other would chop. Working regular that way, we could cut down one, sometimes two trees of a late afternoon. We used the oxen to haul them up near the house.

Then, during the day, when I was at home tending to Father, it was my job to fashion the trees into logs we could use.

First I measured each one for a particular side of the barn. The building was to be just twenty feet across at the front and back, with the sides running only thirty. That meant cutting the trees to those lengths. I used the ax but could not swing it strong enough to cut the trunks into logs the right size. Instead I pounded the ax in with our maul, a kind of wooden club. (I never did tell Harrison or Nettie I needed that maul lest they think me less than them again.)

Next I had to strip off the bark. The trick was to peel it in sheets as big as possible, which we could nail onto the barn roof for shakes. I used Father's peeling chisel, the one with the widest blade. Smaller pieces I used to patch the roof on our house.

Most times I did fine with the peeling, though now and again I nicked myself. Then I would creep inside and bind up with a rag. Only then was I grateful that Father could not notice what I was doing.

Once I had the bark peeled and stacked to dry, I needed to split the length of each tree into halves. I'd start off with a metal wedge, driving it in as close as possible to the centerline of the tree. For that I used the maul again. With the wedge firm and a crack started in the wood, I'd slip in a glut, a sharp pointed stake made of hard oak.

With the maul, I would pound that glut down into the crack, opening it up some more. Then I could yank out the wedge and set it in a bit farther down along the length of the tree. After I drove the wedge in again, I'd set in yet another glut and repeat the whole process all over.

Generally speaking, by the time I drove in five or six gluts, that tree would split right into two fairly even half logs.

Of course by then I was fairly well split with exhaustion myself. That was no problem when I was working alone. But if Nettie or Harrison was about, I had to look to find some sly way to rest. I'd say, "I better go check on Father" or "I think I'll tell Father how we're doing."

No one seemed to mind.

Sometimes Tod Buckman came around to see Nettie. One afternoon he watched me work for a while and then said, "Ben, you're getting to be almost as strong as Harrison."

That pleased me.

"All the same," he added, "I could give you some help. So could others. But Nettie said you say no."

"That's right," I told him. "It has to be just us."

"How do you figure that?"

At first I could not think of an answer. I just looked across the fields.

"Is there that much pride in a barn?" he pressed.

By then I had found my answer. "It isn't just a barn," I said. "It's a gift."

18

Besides wood for the barn, we needed rocks for the foundation. Finding them along the creek run was not hard. But it was another matter to haul them out and bring them up to the site. If we hadn't had the oxen, the chore could hardly have been done.

Once all three of us were fetching stone. It was an unusual hot day. Nettie was lifting a rock, but it slipped and splashed me up fine. Before I thought of what I was doing, I splashed her back. She gave a hoot and splashed me again. Then Harrison joined in. Next thing, we were all splashing away, till we were soaked and laughing to a fit. And who should appear but Tod? Harrison tore out of the creek, grabbed him, and dunked him as well. A rare lark. Nettie, to defend Tod, took after Harrison, whom she and I dunked. And then as a reward, Tod kissed Nettie. I'd never seen him do that. She blushed up pretty when Harrison and I howled. We were all just being children.

19

During these weeks, we kept at our regular tasks. There were the fields to tend, which meant harvesting the wheat crop. Nettie and Harrison took it to town and traded for what we needed. Wheat prices were high that year, and we did prime.

About that time I told Nettie she should write to Mr. Dortmeister and ask him to return the school fees he had kept.

She said, "I don't write well enough for that. Besides, you are going back."

"Not till Father is well," I retorted.

She sighed and looked at Harrison. He said, "There was the promise to Mother."

I only repeated, "Not till Father is well."

"And when will that be?"

"When the barn is up," I said.

No one said anything for a time. Then Harrison turned to Nettie. "We have enough money to wait till then."

She shook her head. "I never heard of a month named Then."

Even so, no more was said about my schooling.

20

All in all we needed eight weeks to take down the trees, haul them out, then cut, trim, and split them, as well as gather foundation stones.

And Father? There was no change other than his gradual wasting away. But since I was getting stronger, it was easier for me to move him about.

After a while, before I worked splitting logs, I would pick him up and ease him into the barrow, then tie him upright so he could see what I was doing. And I talked to him, too. A constant stream. Of course aside from his strange sounds and now and again the blinking of his eyes, he said nothing. But I often acted as if he had talked back to me—had given some advice, shared a story, or even, as he had so often done with me, told a joke.

21

While Nettie and I were still cutting and hauling logs and I was trimming them, Harrison began the notch work. That is, in order to stack the logs up for walls, he had to notch them at both ends.

He decided to do it as simply as possible, which was just a square notch, like cutting a step out from both log ends. He used a mortise ax with the maul. And he did it right, too.

"Where'd you ever learn to do all that?" I questioned.

Harrison nodded over to Father, who was in the barrow, looking on. "I once asked him how come our family moved so much from state to state and then to Oregon Territory. He said the only thing he ever got right was building new houses. That's why we had to keep moving: to keep up his hand. It was his way, he said, of telling the whole country what he *could* do."

We looked at Father, and he blinked at us, as if to say, "Harrison has it right."

It was Nettie's sixteenth birthday. She had forgotten, but Harrison and I had not. He'd carved her a little box, with a lid that was hinged. In the top of it he cut a heart. I baked a sweet cake for her. We gave her these things at supper with Father. Nettie cried and said she would never get married after all. I jumped up and ran for the door.

"What is it?" she asked, alarmed.

"I'm going to tell Tod," I said. We all laughed. I wondered what Father thought of us.

23

In early June, Harrison announced that we had foundation stone and logs enough—stacked, notched, and drying—to start building the barn.

Usually, people putting up a barn got everything ready, then brought in neighbors and worked as a team until it was standing up and roofed. A frolic. We might have done that if we chose. But I wanted the barn to be ours. And Father's.

"We don't know how he'll take to sudden people," I explained one night at dinner. "Other than the three of us and Tod, he's not seen a soul since Dr. Flannagan looked at him four months ago. It might embarrass him."

Nettie disagreed. "I don't remember Father ever being embarrassed."

"But this is different," I said. "And anyway, we should begin on Sunday when we're not in the fields."

"Thought we weren't to work on Sundays," Harrison said. That was a family rule, according to the church Mother and Father had been part of in Vermont.

I said, "I don't think it's work we'll be doing."

"Feels like it," Nettie offered.

I shook my head. "It's not as if we *had* to build a barn. This is a gift for Father. To make him well."

Before they could argue, I left the table to go outside and stand by the logs and the heap of rocks. In my mind's eye, I could see the barn complete. It looked so fine. Better yet was the thought of Father standing right there with me and admiring it, telling me how grand it was.

I lifted one end of a log. Not far, but

hoisting it at all was something I could not have done when I first came back from school. I felt so proud that if it had been just me, I'd have started building right that moment. The sun was still up, the sky all lavender. Sunday was four days off.

24

Two days before we were to begin, Father turned worse. He was tied into his chair, and I had fed him. We were finishing up our own food when he gave this sudden gasp. It was as if the wind had been taken from him. Then his head lolled back, rolled, fell forward.

Taken by surprise, we just looked at him for a moment. Then Nettie sprang up.

"What is it?" Harrison asked.

Nettie drew up Father's head and held it against her chest. His eyes were closed, his mouth slack. For a moment I thought he had died. My heart sank.

"Better get him to bed," Nettie said, and untied Father. He was as limp as a new blanket one minute, then rigid the next.

Harrison carried him. Father lay still, eyes closed. You could see his chest move, but he was having trouble breathing. When I took up one of his hands, it was cold as snow. I chaffed it some, and Nettie did the same with his other hand. Harrison eased off his boots and rubbed his feet.

Then I brought in some wood and heaped the fire till it was roaring. Harrison picked Father up, while Nettie spread a blanket near the hearth. We laid him on it so he could take in some heat.

Finally Nettie sighed. "It's what Dr. Flannagan said might happen: another fit."

We stared at Father and at one another. Then we commenced rubbing him again, and after a while his body seemed to grow less tight. Some warmth came, too, as if he were thawing out.

But there was nothing calm or easy about the way he looked. He had gone thin and gaunt a long time ago, but he was still Father. Now—in a moment—he looked as if a hand had reached into him and cut the threads of his life.

"Is he going to die?" I found the tongue to ask.

"He always was going to," Nettie answered.

"I mean, *soon*?"

"Ben," she whispered. "I don't know."

Harrison asked, "Think I should try to get the doctor?"

Nettie shook her head as if to say, That won't help.

Then I said, "We can't wait for Sunday."

"What are you talking about?" Nettie snapped.

I said, "We have to start building the barn."

"Please, Ben!" she cried out, shaking her head again. "Don't go on so!"

"We have to," I said. "We do! He has to have it."

Harrison said, "I don't think he has to have anything."

"But we promised we'd do it!" I cried.

Nettie rebuked me sharply: "No one promised anything."

"I did," I replied. "Harrison was there. And Father agreed."

"Agreed to what?"

"Getting better if we built the barn."

"Is that true?" Nettie asked Harrison.

He looked away. "It's what Ben said."

Nettie sat down on a chair, pressing her hands to her face.

"We could call in Tod," Harrison offered. "Or even the Gartells."

"No," I insisted, "it must be just us."

"Ben, you exhaust me more than Father." Nettie turned from us, but we stood there looking at her.

I said, "It's going to make him better."

She shuddered.

"It will!" I insisted.

Finally Nettie gave a small lift to her shoulders. I knew then that she had given way and that Harrison would follow.

25

By sunup next morning, we were ready. I tried to feed Father, but it was futile. He would take no food. Nor did he make a response of any kind. All we could do was heap up the fire, make sure he was warm, then leave him on his bed.

Outside, Harrison was in charge. We needed him to be, because Nettie and I had only a small notion as to what was to be done. But under Harrison's instruction, we began by digging a shallow trench along the four lines of the barn, the exception being the five feet marking the door. Then he and Nettie hauled in big rocks and began laying them in that trench for the foundation.

Of course to make those stones set right, to make a level foundation, was no easy task. It took much lifting and chopping out of bits of earth, as well as filling some back in. Often the rocks themselves had to be chipped. Harrison was forever resetting stones, casting his eye upon their lines this way, then that way.

I was all for saying, All that matters is getting the barn built; but I knew that was wrong and that Harrison had to do it properly. Actually he sounded much like Mr. Dortmeister, constantly saying that if the foundation was not solid, nothing else would stand. He meant it, too.

While he and Nettie were wrestling the big rocks into the trench, I filled chinks with smaller stones. To smooth it off, I hauled mud up from the creek, crumbled in tiny bits of branch, and stuffed this wattle and daub in the cracks.

That first day we did not leave off until nightfall took our eyes, but even so, it was two and a half days before Harrison said the foundation was complete.

"We should show it to Father."

"He can't see it, Ben," Nettie answered.

"Maybe he can feel it," I suggested.

"No!" she said.

I did not argue but next day started off by dragging our table outside and putting Father on it. Whether he knew what we were doing we couldn't tell. But there seemed to be some improvement in his condition. That is, I was able to get some food into him, a thin mash of ground wheat and milk. Now and again—if you could catch it—his eyes would open. But his cheeks were more diminished. His color stayed gray. All in all, his state was a discouragement.

26

With the foundation set, the real barn building could begin. Harrison told us which log to start with. Nettie and I roped it and tied it to the ox yoke, and the great beasts dragged it to the foundation. Then the three of us lifted it, pushed it, and finally set it in place on the rocks, flat side out. The first log was down.

Excited, I ran to Father and shouted, "The barn is going up!" I would have given much for the quick blink of an eye but saw not a flicker.

The farm work that should have been tended to was ignored, though we did milk the cow. The mule was set to pasture. Otherwise we worked on the barn from early morning till late at night. It was my idea to light a fire in the very center of the rectangle. There being no roof yet, there was no danger, and the light the fire cast enabled us to work longer hours.

Slowly the barn began to rise. By the end of the first week—working as hard as we could—we had the walls up. The front wall was higher than the others so as to give the flat roof a slant down toward the west. Harrison had said the winds usually blew from that direction.

Next came the putting up of the roof beams, their highest point at the front, their lowest along the rear wall. Harrison chose the strongest wood we had, but not so strong as to be heavy beyond our ability to lift it.

They sent me to straddle the top of the front wall, rope in hand. The other end was tied to the beam we were hoisting. With Nettie and Harrison doing the lifting and me guiding and pulling, we inched the first log up bit by bit. Once we managed to hang it over the front wall, we then heaved the other end over the back.

Throughout, Father was by us on the table, somewhat propped up, but giving no signs.

Harrison wanted six beams for the roof, and the raising of those six beams took a whole day. But at last the framing was complete.

No sooner was it done than I reminded him how each time Father had built a house, he'd stuck on a small tree at the top once the frame was up. When I had asked him why he did that, he told me he was signaling the Lord that he wouldn't build any higher so as to get into heaven the easy way. This time, it was Harrison who set the tree on the top.

"The tree is up!" I shouted into Father's ear. There was no more response than before.

The rest of the roof went quickly. Over those long, sloping beams we laid small, thin trees crossways in long rows, from the rear on up to the top. Then we wattled them over, finally laying down the bark sheets I had prepared.

It was dark when Harrison pronounced the barn complete. Father had long since been put to bed inside the house. So we three stood in the faint glow from the door and looked at what we had built. It was nothing much to look at and probably not truly square. Yet it was bigger than anything we had done before. It seemed to say, "We are here. We will stay."

With Nettie and Harrison behind me, I rushed into the house and I ran up to Father's bed. "The barn is done!" I cried. Though he stirred somewhat, he seemed to be asleep. So I turned to Nettie and Harrison and said, "We'll tell him tomorrow."

Next morning I was awake first, bubbling with excitement. Even though our windows were poor, I could see it was going to be a fine, bright day, just right for what was about to happen. I felt all puffed out.

My first thought was to clean and dress Father before the others woke. I longed to give him some sense of what we had done, to win perhaps some small recognition.

Making sure I did not wake Harrison, I slipped down from our loft and crept over to where Father lay in his bed. The instant I saw him, I realized that in the night he had died.

For the longest time, I simply stood by his side and stared at him. His mouth was agape, his eyes closed, his fingers no longer scratching at his coverlet. I saw no mark of peace upon him, no look of release.

Gazing down, I tried to find my grief. To my horror all I found was anger.

"Father!" I burst out. "You should have waited for me to give you the barn! You promised! It's not fair!"

Then, realizing what I had said, I fled from the house in shame and ran to the farthest corner of our claim, down to the creek. When I reached it, I flung myself into its low, cold waters, rolling this way and that over mud and stones to wash away my sin.

When I could no longer bear the chill, I stood up and—shivering in the morning air—hurled myself on the bank and there gave way to grief.

My sister and brother found me some while later. Nettie gathered me up into her lap. I sobbed and sobbed. Harrison rested a hand on my back.

Though I cried myself to rags, they

never said a word. Not until I sat up. "Ben," Harrison said then, "we knew it was coming."

"No," I answered with a shake of my head. "It's not that."

"What, then?" Nettie asked.

"I did a terrible thing."

"What?" Harrison said.

"When I found him, my only thought was that he wasn't fair to us."

"Ben," Nettie said, "Father never could go anywhere but he was too soon or too late. The same for our building the barn. He couldn't stay for the giving."

I shook my head and said, "I wasn't building it for him."

"Who for, then?" Harrison asked.

"It was for me—for *me* to give to him. So he would thank *me*. Be grateful to *me*. So he'd see I wasn't different."

Nettie grew all quiet. Then she said, "Don't you see, Ben, that proves he *must* have known what we did."

"Why?"

"What was the last thing you said last night?"

I thought awhile, and then I said, "It was when we came inside. I said that the barn was done."

She said, "He must have heard and understood."

I said, "What do you mean?"

"Ben, he could not bear taking the barn without giving you something in return. But what had he to give? Nothing. So he chose to go rather than show you that. To hide his failure, that was *his* gift."

"Look, Ben," Harrison said, "if it weren't for him getting sick, you'd never have talked us into building that barn. You kept saying *he* wanted it. Don't you see—it was *his* gift to you."

There it was, then: a choice. Did I build the barn for myself? Did we build it for Father? Or did Father get me to build it for us all?

Or was it all three at once?

28

Harrison rode for the minister, but he was out on circuit, so we did Father's service ourselves.

Harrison and I built the coffin. Nettie dressed Father proper and laid him out. Then we went to the hill where Mother was buried and laid him next to her.

I read from our Bible the same prayer that Mr. Dortmeister had read when I had left his school: "Our Father, who art in heaven."

As Nettie, Harrison, and I came back down to the house, down from the hill, and saw the barn before us, we stopped and could not help but gaze upon it. After all the work it took to make, all that time and effort, it seemed—sitting there in our acres—hardly more than a blade of grass in a field of wheat. And yet it was the only thing we saw.

I said, "When I was reading that 'Our Father,' I wasn't thinking of any God. I was thinking of *our* father and wondering where he was. And then I thought that if Father is anywhere, he's in that barn."

To which both Nettie and Harrison said, "Amen."

29

It is almost seventy years since that time. But every morning when I get up, the first thing I do is look at the barn. Like Father promised: it's something fine to come home to. Still standing. Still strong.